To Evan & Ava,

Just be you! :)

Just Me, Wrigley

Savy Leiser

Just Me, Wrigley

Written & Illustrated

by Savy Leiser

For every art teacher I've ever had.

- Savy

Foreword

A *forever home* is exactly what it sounds like: a home you can live in forever, with a family that will always love you unconditionally. Unfortunately, many dogs struggle to find their forever homes. After experiencing abuse or neglect by previous owners, dogs can end up in shelters, in foster homes, or sometimes as strays. As these dogs roam from place to place, they all have one wish: to find a family that will love them forever.

The Furever Home Friends series presents the stories of real dogs who have lived such lives. Some of these dogs have found their forever homes, and some are still looking. For every dog in these books, there are thousands more waiting for someone to give them the family they deserve.

Wrigley is so happy that you decided to welcome her into your heart. She can't wait to be your new Friend Furever.

I am a dancing dog!
I can hop and bop.
I can wiggle and wriggle.

That's why my name is Wrigley!

I love to shake my tail all over the
animal shelter!

But lately, I've been worried that
my dancing isn't helping me get
adopted.

At my first house, I was a Christmas present.

On Christmas morning, I popped out of my box and started dancing to "Jingle Bells!"

"What kinda dog is this?" asked the boy.

"A dancing dog, it seems!" laughed the mom.

"But what kind? What breed?" asked the boy.

"I don't know," sighed the mom. "But isn't she cute?"

"I wanted a Dalmatian," said the boy.

The next day, that mom put me into her minivan. Hooray! A ride in the car! I stuck my face out the window and enjoyed the feeling of the breeze against my long, thick fur. That's when I saw where we were going: back to the animal shelter.

After I was handed back over to a shelter volunteer, I heard the mom ask, "Do you guys have any Dalmatians?"

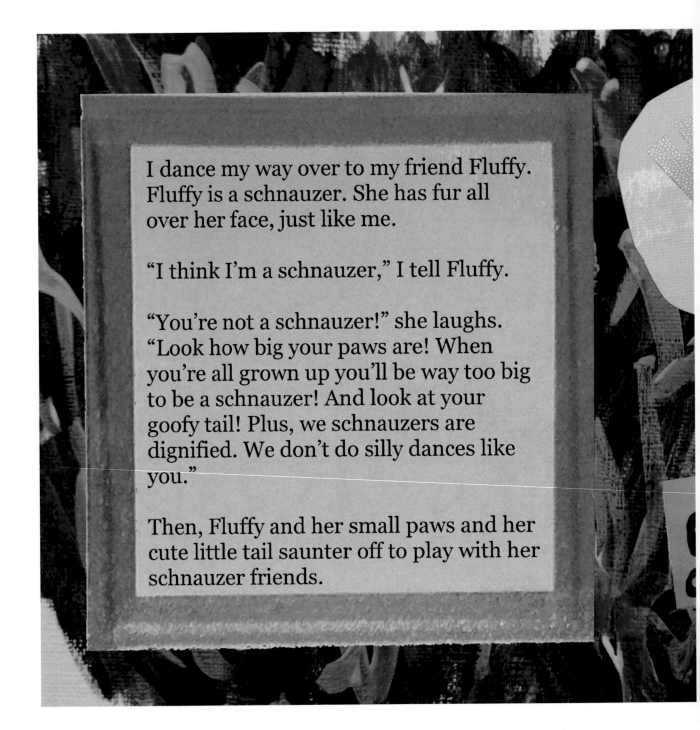

I dance my way over to my friend Fluffy. Fluffy is a schnauzer. She has fur all over her face, just like me.

"I think I'm a schnauzer," I tell Fluffy.

"You're not a schnauzer!" she laughs. "Look how big your paws are! When you're all grown up you'll be way too big to be a schnauzer! And look at your goofy tail! Plus, we schnauzers are dignified. We don't do silly dances like you."

Then, Fluffy and her small paws and her cute little tail saunter off to play with her schnauzer friends.

My friend Frank is a black lab. He has dark fur and big floppy ears like me. I dance my way over to Frank, only to trip on my own two paws, and fall right on my face! Maybe Fluffy's right; my paws are too big!

"I think I'm a black lab," I tell Frank. He bursts out laughing at me too! "You're not a black lab! Look at your scraggly monkey fur! And your fur isn't even all black! Plus, you just fell on your face! Labs are athletic. We don't do silly dances like you."

Then Frank runs off to play ball with his lab friends.

When a young couple comes to the shelter, I saunter around the playground, looking pretty like Fluffy.

Except I trip over my big paws.

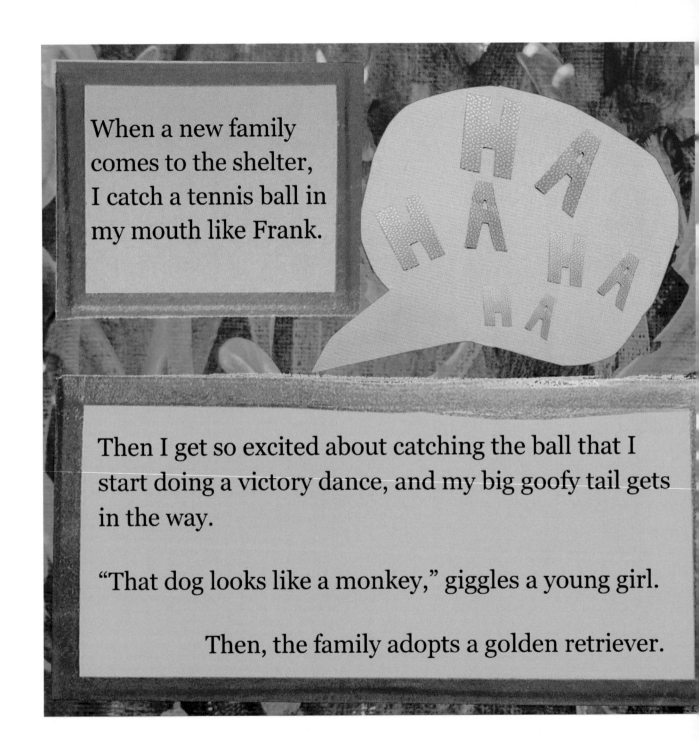

When a new family comes to the shelter, I catch a tennis ball in my mouth like Frank.

Then I get so excited about catching the ball that I start doing a victory dance, and my big goofy tail gets in the way.

"That dog looks like a monkey," giggles a young girl.

Then, the family adopts a golden retriever.

This is ridiculous! I am trying so hard to be like the other dogs, and still no one is noticing me!

Today, there is a man at the shelter. He has a friendly smile. "What kind of dog are you looking for?" a shelter volunteer asks him.

"A fun one!" he says.

ADOPTION PAPER

NAME _Wrigley_

BREED ?

I start dancing right there in my crate.

I **hop** and **bop**. I **wiggle** and **wriggle**.

And the man looks right at me!

"She looks fun!" he says.
"That's Wrigley. She's a big goofball," laughs the volunteer.

Then, she grabs the adoption papers!

When we reach our new home, my new dad puts some rock and roll on the radio.

I start **hopping** and **bopping** and **wiggling** and **wriggling**.

He grabs my paws and we dance the night away!

My dad doesn't know what breed I am, and he may never know. I may never know, either.

What I do know is that I'm just me. Wrigley.

The dancing dog!

Wrigley's Discussion Questions

for Kids, Parents, and Dogs!

1) Even though Wrigley has a home at the beginning of the story, she ends up back at the shelter. What could the first family have done differently so that this didn't happen?

2) How do you think Wrigley feels when she tries to fit in with the schnauzers and labs at the shelter, only to be rejected? Have you ever felt like you didn't fit in with a group? What can you do to overcome those feelings?

3) Wrigley doesn't know what breed she is. In reality, Wrigley is probably a mix of many different dog breeds. What challenges might mixed-breed dogs face as opposed to purebred dogs? What similar struggles might people face?

4) Wrigley loves to dance! Dancing makes her different from the other dogs at the shelter, but it's also what makes her special. What are your special talents and interests?

5) When Wrigley wants to be like the other dogs at the shelter, she stops dancing—but in the end, her dancing helps her find her forever home! When is a time you chose to stay true to yourself rather than following the crowd? What happened as a result?

Meet Wrigley

in Real Life!

Wrigley is a mutt of unknown origin living in the north suburbs of Chicago. She loves dancing with her dad and causing general mischief!

When Wrigley was a young puppy, her first family returned her to the shelter. Soon after, she was adopted again by her forever family. Wrigley's family, the shelter volunteers, and the vet have all guessed that she might be a different breed—from a schnauzer, to a terrier, to part lab. But no one knows for sure, and her family is fine with keeping it that way!

You can visit Wrigley and the other dogs online at fureverhomefriends.com/the-dogs.

About the Author & Illustrator

Savy Leiser is a Chicago author, journalist, artist, and freelance editor. Savy earned her Bachelor's Degree from Northwestern University in 2015, and remains a devoted Wildcats fan, even though she's currently pursuing her Master's in Writing and Publishing at DePaul University.

When she's not working on *Furever Home Friends* books, Savy embraces her alter-ego as a young-adult and new-adult author. Her first young-adult book, *The Making of a Small-Town Beauty King*, released in February 2016, and her first new-adult novel, *Sculpt Yourself*, will release in November of 2018.

Savy also writes for *Halftime Magazine* and teaches creative writing workshops at Open Books. *Just Me, Wrigley* is the first book that Savy has illustrated.

You can visit Savy online at savyleiser.com.

Acknowledgments

Thank you to all of our Kickstarter backers who pledged to make our first two books, *Princess Allee* and *Smile, Chewie!*, possible.

We would also like to thank the Coleman Entrepreneurship Center at DePaul University for all of your support in the process of expanding the Furever Home Friends as a series and as a business. We'd like to also give a shout-out to DePaul's University Center for Writing-based Learning for all of their support as well.

Additionally, thank you to every critique group member who looked over this book's many drafts before it reached this point. Your valuable feedback helped this book reach its final form!

Finally, Savy would like to thank every art teacher she's ever had—but Heidi Benson and Ozge Samanci in particular—for teaching her the color theory and digital art techniques that inspired her to illustrate this book. She was super nervous about illustrating a book for the first time, but now has something she can be proud of!

Other Books in this Series

1. *Princess Allee*
2. *Smile, Chewie!*

Get a signed copy of all our books on
fureverhomefriends.com!

If you enjoyed this book, please consider leaving a review on
Amazon or Goodreads!

74036221R00022

Made in the USA
Columbia, SC
10 September 2019